DATE			

AQUARIUM
ADMIT ONE

Oliver's Otter Phase

by Lisa Connors

illustrated by Karen Jones

Oliver's otter phase

began one morning after a trip to the aquarium.

We arrived at the aquarium!

At breakfast, Oliver chewed his
eggs and toast . . .

. . . slowly,

. . . carefully.

"Dad, don't gulp! Otters chew their food."

"But I'm not an otter," said Dad.

"I am,"

Oliver said.

We found the otter exhibit.

Oliver loves the otters!

At lunch, Oliver took apart his bologna sandwich, lifted up his shirt, and slapped his bologna on his chest.

"Oliver, what are you doing?" Mom asked.

"Using my body as a plate.
That's what otters do,"
Oliver said.

Otter dinner time!

He picked up the bologna, took a
bite and chewed . . .

. . . slowly,

. . . carefully.

"I didn't know otters liked bologna
sandwiches," Mom replied.

"Your otter does,"
Oliver said.

sea urchins & mussels

a young sea otter

He finished his sandwich,

slid out of his chair,

and squirmed off to play.

Otters like to dive.

Later, Oliver went to the grocery store with his Dad. When Dad lifted him into the shopping cart seat, Oliver handed him a long string.

"Otter moms tie their babies to a long piece of kelp so they don't get lost when she goes hunting."

"But I'm not an otter's mom," Dad said, winking.

Otters hold kelp.

At dinner, Oliver tried to slap his spaghetti on his bare stomach, but it was still hot . . .

and messy!

He was so busy catching
it from falling

he forgot to chew slowly.

Strong teeth crack shells.

This one is friendly!

"I think my otter needs a bath right away," Mom said.

"Otters love baths!"

Guess what Oliver picked?

Oliver snuck a cookie into his armpit, slid off the chair, and **wiggled** up to the bath.

underarm pouch

When Oliver raised his arms to wash his hair, his cookie fell into the water. "Oops, my pocket must have a hole." Oliver frowned. "Other otters store food in their underarm pocket."

"Well, otters don't eat cookie treats anyway," Mom said. "Help me fish out the crumbs."

"Otters don't eat a lot of fish. They love clams and sea urchins," Oliver said.

otter grooming

expert swimmers

"Hmm," said Mom, "I'd rather have a cookie."
"And bologna sandwiches!" Oliver said.

Oliver splashed around a bit.
"I'm ready to get out."

Otters "hold hands."

"Is my otter all clean and dry?" Mom asked, helping Oliver with his pajamas.

"I think I want to stop being an otter. Except for one very special thing."

"What's that?"
Mom asked.

Oliver is tired!

He fell asleep.

Slowly . . .

carefully . . .

Oliver crawled into his mom's lap.

"THIS!"

Otter snuggles

For Creative Minds

Marine Mammals

a mammal . . .

- is an animal
- has a backbone
- breathes oxygen from the air
- is warm-blooded
- has hair
- feeds milk to its young

Most mammals (but not all!) give birth to live young.

Not all animals with backbones are mammals, but all mammals have backbones.

Can you think of any animals with backbones that are *not* mammals?

There are many animals that share some traits of a mammal. But only a mammal has *all* of these traits.

Are *you* a mammal?

Are you a *marine* mammal?

A **marine mammal** is a mammal that is adapted to spend all or most of its life in the ocean. There are more than a hundred different species of marine mammals! Seals, sea lions, whales, dolphins, porpoises, manatees, dugongs, sea otters, walruses, and polar bears are some of the different types of marine mammals.

Sea otters live in the northern Pacific Ocean. They spend almost their entire lives in the water, but sometimes come onto land to rest, groom, or nurse their young.

The water is very cold, so sea otters need a way to stay warm. Most marine mammals have a thick layer of fat, called blubber, that helps keep their body warm. But not sea otters! Instead they have thick fur. Sea otters have the densest fur of any mammal.

Sea otters are smaller than humans, but not by much! Adult sea otters are 3-5 feet long. Most humans are about 5-6 feet tall. But by marine mammal standards, sea otters are pretty puny. The largest marine mammal is the blue whale. At almost 100 feet long, its not just the biggest marine mammal, it's the biggest living animal in the world!

Are you taller than a sea otter is long? Are any sea otters longer than you?

Sea Otters and You

sea otter	human
mammal	mammal
chews food	chews food
eats food with paws	eats food with hands
uses tools	uses tools
has two paws and two flippers	has two hands and two feet
lives in water	lives on land
has hair	has hair
torpedo-shaped body for swimming	upright body for walking on two feet
has a skin pocket under their arms to hold rocks or carry food	wears clothes with pockets to carry things
grooms hair	grooms hair
has whiskers	sometimes has whiskers

Otters use teeth called "molars" to chew. Molars are large teeth with a flat surface.

Open your mouth and say "Aaahhh!" Are there any molars in your mouth?

Otters' whiskers sense vibrations to help them hunt.

Otters have 170,000 to 1 million hairs per square inch on their bodies. Humans have only about 100,000 hairs on their whole bodies!

one square inch

All that hair needs a lot of attention. Otters spend 2-3 hours each day grooming their hair. How much time do you spend taking care of your hair?

Some people have whiskers. On humans, we usually call them beards or mustaches.

Sea Otter Tools

Sea otters use tools in many ways! People use tools too. Does Oliver use tools the way an otter does? Match the sea otter's skill to Oliver's.

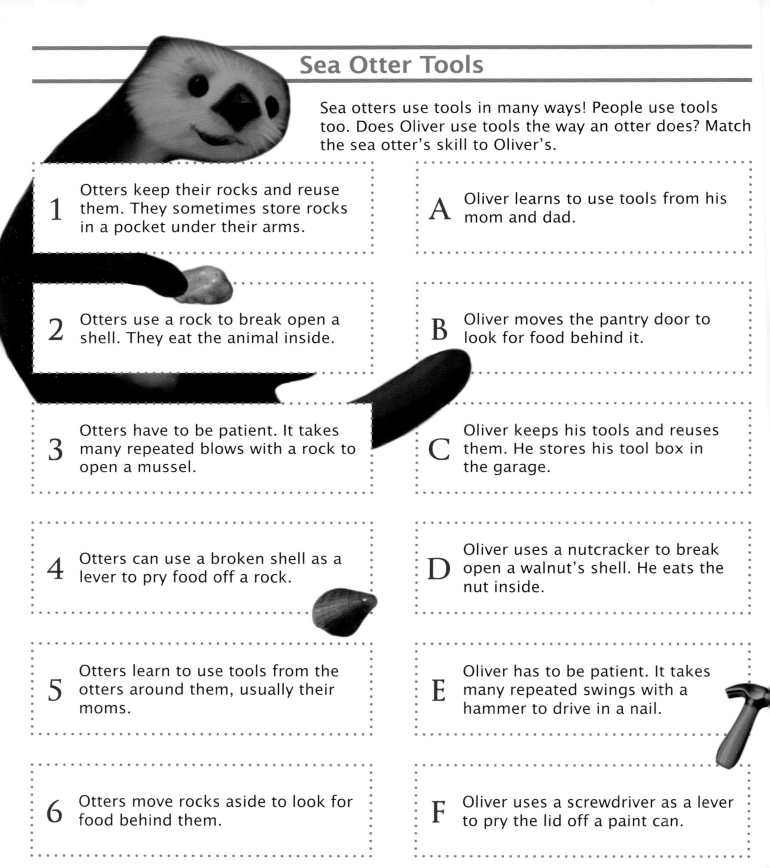

1 Otters keep their rocks and reuse them. They sometimes store rocks in a pocket under their arms.

A Oliver learns to use tools from his mom and dad.

2 Otters use a rock to break open a shell. They eat the animal inside.

B Oliver moves the pantry door to look for food behind it.

3 Otters have to be patient. It takes many repeated blows with a rock to open a mussel.

C Oliver keeps his tools and reuses them. He stores his tool box in the garage.

4 Otters can use a broken shell as a lever to pry food off a rock.

D Oliver uses a nutcracker to break open a walnut's shell. He eats the nut inside.

5 Otters learn to use tools from the otters around them, usually their moms.

E Oliver has to be patient. It takes many repeated swings with a hammer to drive in a nail.

6 Otters move rocks aside to look for food behind them.

F Oliver uses a screwdriver as a lever to pry the lid off a paint can.

Answers: 1-C, 2-D, 3-E, 4-F, 5-A, 6-B

Sea Otters and River Otters

Sea Otters

- weigh 50-100 pounds
- have thick, brown fur. The fur on their heads and paws gets lighter as they get older
- have a flattened tail, less than a third of their body length
- live in salt water along rocky coastlines, often in kelp forests
- float on their backs
- grab food with flexible paws
- eat food on their chests as they float
- sleep wrapped in kelp
- have just one pup at a time
- eat mostly urchins, crabs, clams, mussels, snails and octopuses
- gather together to make a group of otters called a raft

- are a type of weasel
- have long torpedo-shaped bodies
- are meat-eaters (carnivores)
- have webbed feet for swimming
- have claws
- have two layers of fur to keep warm

River Otters

- weigh 20-25 pounds
- have fur that can be grey and white to brown and black
- have a rounded tail, more than half their body length
- live in freshwater rivers, ponds, lakes, and wetlands (including estuaries)
- swim on their bellies
- catch prey with their paws and mouth
- eat food on land
- sleep in underground dens
- have two or three pups at a time—or sometimes as many as six!
- eat fish, frogs, crayfish, insects, rats, and birds

A special thanks to Chris for the gift of time.—LC

For my professors, classmates and students at NCSU College of Design—KJ

Thanks to Cathleen McConnell at Point Defiance Zoo & Aquarium for verifying the accuracy of the information in this book.

Library of Congress Cataloging-in-Publication Data

Names: Connors, Lisa, 1965- author. | Lee, Karen (Karen Jones), 1961- illustrator.
Title: Oliver's otter phase / by Lisa Connors ; illustrated by Karen Jones.
Description: Mount Pleasant, SC : Arbordale Publishing, [2018] | Summary: After a trip to the aquarium, Oliver decides to be an otter and tries to copy otter behavior at meals, while playing, during a trip to the store, and at bath time.
Identifiers: LCCN 2017040944 (print) | LCCN 2017049366 (ebook) | ISBN 9781607184843 (English Downloadable eBook) | ISBN 9781607185154 (English Interactive Dual-Language eBook) | ISBN 9781607184898 (Spanish Downloadable eBook) | ISBN 9781607185208 (Spanish Interactive Dual-Language eBook) | ISBN 9781607184515 (english hardcover) | ISBN 9781607184621 (english pbk.) | ISBN 9781607184676 (spanish pbk.)
Subjects: | CYAC: Otters--Fiction.
Classification: LCC PZ7.1.C6473 (ebook) | LCC PZ7.1.C6473 Ol 2018 (print) | DDC [E]--dc23
LC record available at https://lccn.loc.gov/2017040944

Translated into Spanish: *Nico: Nutria por un dia*

Lexile® Level: 550L

key phrases: sea otters, otters, animal adaptations, marine mammals

Bibliography:
Brody, Allan. Personal communication with the author about Dr. Brody's work with sea otters for his PhD from the University of Minnesota, 2014.
Garshelis, Dave. Personal Communication with the author about Dr. Garshelis' work with sea otters in Alaska, through the University of Minnesota. 2014.
Knight. "Motherhood Is No Picnic for Sea Otter Moms." *Journal of Experimental Biology* (2014): n. pag. Web.
Thometz. "Energetic Demands of Immature Sea Otters from Birth to Weaning: Implications for Maternal Costs, Reproductive Behavior and Population-level Trends." *Journal of Experimental Biology* (n.d.): n. pag. Web.
"Sea Otter." *The Marine Mammal Center.* N.p., n.d. Web. 19 Oct. 2016.
"Spotlight on Sea Otters." *Vancouver Aquarium.* N.p., n.d. Web. 4 Jan. 2015.

7459